For My Little Family-
Every day, now and always, all my love. XO!
- N. B.

With love to Louise and Eloise
- J. L.

tiger tales
5 River Road, Suite 128, Wilton, CT 06897
Published in the United States 2016
Originally published in Great Britain 2016
by Little Tiger Press
Text copyright © 2016 Nicky Benson
Illustrations copyright © 2016 Jonny Lambert
ISBN-13: 978-1-68010-022-8
ISBN-10: 1-68010-022-X
Printed in China
LTP/1800/1244/0915

For more insight and activities, visit us at
www.tigertalesbooks.com

I Love You More and More

by Nicky Benson

Illustrated by Jonny Lambert

tiger tales

You are my everything,
I love you high and low.

I love you more than flowers
love to blossom, bloom, and grow.

I love you more than trees love to change with every season.

I love you more than anything,

I cannot name just one reason.

I love you more than waterfalls
love to splash on me and you.

I love you more than fish
love to swirl in rivers blue.

I love you more than mountains
love the clouds breezing by.

I love you more than stars
love to sparkle in the sky.

You are beautiful in all you do,
and in all the words you say—

I love you, baby, more and more
with every precious day.